B
Q

PATRICK SÜSKIND

Maître Mussard's Bequest

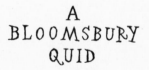

A
BLOOMSBURY
QUID

Das Vermächtnis des Maître Mussard (1975)
first published in *Neu Deutsche Hefte, No.149*,
Berlin 1976

This edition © 1996
Copyright © 1976, 1996 by Patrick Süskind and
© 1995 by Diogenes Verlag AG Zürich
Translation © 1995 by Irving Wardle

Bloomsbury Publishing Plc,
2 Soho Square, London W1V 6HB

A CIP catalogue record for this book
is available from the British Library

ISBN 0 7475 2894 2

Typeset by Hewer Text Composition Services,
Edinburgh
Printed by St Edmundsbury Press, Suffolk
Jacket design by Jeff Fisher

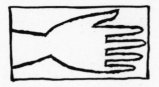

Ceaselessly occupied with his curious discoveries, Mussard worked himself into such a fever over these thoughts that they would eventually have entangled his mind in madness, had not death torn him away from them by a strange and cruel illness: luckily for his reason, but not for his sorrowing friends to whom he was dear and valued.

Rousseau, *Confessions*

These few pages are addressed to some unknown reader of a later age who has the courage to face the truth and the strength to bear it. The feeble-spirited may flee my words like fire, for I have nothing comforting to impart. I must make haste for I have but a short time left to live. The mere act of writing a few sentences demands a super-human exertion, which would be far beyond me, but for an inner compulsion that drives me to pass on my knowledge and its implications to the future world.

The doctors say I am suffering from *Paralysis stomachosa*, but the source of this malady is known only to me. It consists of a rapidly developing paralysis of my limbs and inner organs. Night and day it compels me to sit bolt upright in bed, supported by cushions, with a writing pad on the blanket by my left hand – the right hand being completely immovable. Turning the pages is the task of my faithful servant

Manet, to whom I have bequeathed the care of my estate. For three weeks I have taken only liquid nourishment, and for the past two days even swallowing a mouthful of water causes intolerable pain. But I must not dwell any longer on my present condition. I must devote all my remaining strength to describing my discovery. First of all, a few words about myself.

Jean-Jacques Mussard. I was born in Genf on 12 March 1687. My father was a shoemaker; but I soon found myself aspiring towards some higher trade, and became apprenticed to a goldsmith. After several years I took the journeyman's examination. The work I submitted – such is the mockery of fate – was a ruby set in a golden shell. After two years of travelling, seeing the Alps, the ocean, and the spacious lands between them, I settled in Paris where I found a place with the goldsmith, Maître Lambert, in the rue Verdelet. His early death left me temporarily in charge of his workshop; and a year later I married his widow, thus attaining the rank of Master with full Guild rights. Over the next twenty years I succeeded in transforming the modest little establishment in the rue Verdelet into the largest and most respected jeweller's shop in the whole of Paris. My clients came from the city's most distinguished houses and from the best families in the land with Court connections. My rings, brooches, and diadems found their way into Holland, England, Germany. Many a crowned head crossed my threshold. In 1733, two years after the death of my beloved wife, I had the honour to be appointed Court Jeweller to the Duke of Orleans.

Admission into the most brilliant circles of our society was not without its effect on my intellectual development and the growth of my character.

I learned from the conversations to which I became accustomed, and from books to which I devoted my every spare minute. By such means, over the years, I acquired so fundamental an understanding of science, literature, and art that, although I had never attended a senior school or university, I could style myself without arrogance as a learned man. I mingled in all the leading salons, and received some of the most celebrated spirits of the age as my guests: Diderot, Dondillac, d'Alembert sat at my table. The correspondence I enjoyed for some years with Voltaire will be found among my posthumous papers. I counted even the retiring Rousseau among my friends.

I do not record these details with the aim of impressing my future reader – should he exist – with a roll-call of famous names. Rather do I seek to avoid reproaches when I come to reveal my unbelievable discoveries. It might be alleged that I am a poor fool whose claims are not be be taken seriously, coming from a scientific and philosophic ignoramus. I invoke those men as witnesses to the clarity of my intellect and my strength of judgment. To anyone who sees no reason to take me seriously, I have this to say: Who are you, my friend, to contradict a man whom the greatest of his time respected as an equal?

The enlargement of the workshop and extension of my business had made me a wealthy man. Yet, the older I became, the less enchantment gold and precious stones held for me, and the more I prized my books and scientific studies. And so, well before my sixtieth year, I resolved to withdraw from business life and pass my remaining days in prosperous retirement from the bustle of the capital. With this aim, I acquired a piece of land in the neighbourhood of Passy, where I had a spacious house built together with a garden planted with a rich variety of ornamental bushes, flower-beds, fruit trees, as well as neat gravel paths and watery ways. The whole retreat was separated from the outer world by a thick boxtree hedge. In its alluring tranquillity it seemed a fitting place for a man to enjoy a few years of peace and pleasure between the cares of living and the moment of death. On 22 May 1742, at the the age of fifty-five, I moved from Paris to Passy and embarked on my new existence.

Oh! When I think now of the happiness and quiet joy of that spring day when I arrived at Passy. When I think of the same night and of going to bed for the first time in my life without the expectation of waking up to another day of toil, delivery dates, rush and anxiety. With no sound but the rustling of the alders in own garden, how sweetly I slept – on the same cushion on which I now sit like a stone. I do not know whether to curse or bless that day. Since then, my path has been one of gradual self-destruction, leading to my present wretched state. But since then, too, the truth has been unveiled to me, piece by piece; the truth of the beginning, the course, and the end of our life, our world, and of our whole cosmos. The face of truth is terrible, and its gaze as deadly as the Head of Medusa. But, whether by accident or tireless searching, whoever finds the road towards it must pursue that road to the end – even though this will bring him neither peace nor comfort, nor any man's thanks.

At this point, my unknown reader, pause and examine yourself before you read any further. Are you strong enough to hear the worst of all? What I have to tell you exceeds the outrageous, and when once I have opened your eyes, you will see a new world and will no longer see the old. The new world will be hateful. It will bring oppression, distress, and torment. Stifle all expectation of any remaining hope, escape, or comfort – beyond the comfort that now you know the truth, and that the truth is final. Read no more if you fear the truth. Lay these pages aside if finality awakens your dread. Flee my words, if you cherish the peace of your soul. There is no shame in ignorance; to most of us it counts as happiness. It is, after all, the only possible happiness this world has to offer. Reflect before you throw it away!

What I now have to say to you is something you will never forget, for in your innermost heart you know it already – just as I knew it before it became obvious to me. We have only struggled against the impulse to acknowledge and express it: *The World*, I tell you, *is a shell that mercilessly closes-in on itself.*

Are you resisting me? Are you trying to defend yourself against that insight? No wonder. It is too big a step. One cannot make it all at once. The fog of ages is too thick to be dispersed by one great stroke of light. Instead we need a hundred little lamps. So I will resume the story of my life, and in this way you may gradually come to share in the enlightenment that befell me.

I have already described the garden

that surrounded my new home. In reality, it was a small park, containing a multitude of rare flowers, shrubs, and trees. But, above all, I had it planted with simple roses, as the sight of a blossoming rose has always made a calming and comforting impression on me. I had given my gardener a free hand in matters of detail, and the good man, meaning to please me, had laid out a wide border of roses on the west-facing side of the house. He could not have guessed that, however much I liked looking at roses, I had no liking for them in rampant proliferation. Even less could he have guessed that the laying out of that flower-bed marked the beginning of a new and final chapter in the history of the human race. As for the roses, nothing could

make them thrive. Their stems re-
mained wretchedly small, many with-
ering despite the most industrious
watering, and while the rest of the
garden came splendidly into bloom,
the roses outside my western windows
hardly put out a single bud. I discussed
this with the gardener, whose only
advice was to dig up the whole bed,
and replant it with fresh soil. This
struck me as a cumbersome solution,
and as I was privately none too happy at
having the roses so near to the house, I
decided to uproot the whole border,
and replace it with a terrace adjoining
my salon, from which one might enjoy
a view of the whole garden and admire
the beauties of the sunset. I was so
taken with this idea that I resolved to
execute it myself.

I began by removing the rose trees and turning the earth, so that it could then be filled with gravel and sand as an underlay for paving stones. But after a few spade strokes I found I was no longer digging up loose earth. Instead I struck against a tough whitish stratum that made digging much harder. I took a pick-axe as a help to loosening it. It crumbled under the blows and broke up into small pieces which I dug up and put to one side. My specialist interest in this unfamiliar rock was reduced by the irritation of extra work, until my gaze fell on the loaded shovel I was about to empty. I saw a fist-sized stone, and a finely shaped object which seemed to be glued to its side. I put the spade down and took the stone in my hand, realising with amazement that this shapely object on the side of the stone was a petrified shell. At this point, I stopped work and went into the house to investigate my find. The shell appeared to have grown fixedly into the stone, and was hardly to be distinguished from it even by colour, as it shared the same pattern of white, yellow, and grey, which alternately deepened and splayed out like a fan, emphasising the raised grain. It was the size of a *louis d'or*, and its exterior was identical to the shells you find on the beaches of Normandy and Brittany, which form a popular lunch dish. When I took a knife and scraped the shell so as to break its surface, I found that there was no difference between that scratch and a scratch anywhere on the stone itself. I ground the broken-off

piece of shell in one mortar and a piece
of stone in another; both produced the
same greyish-white powder. When
mixed with a few drops of water, it
resembled the paint used for white-
washing walls. The shell and the stone
both consisted of one and the same
substance. At first I did not fully grasp
the monstrous implications of this
finding. I was too taken by what I
supposed to be a unique discovery,
believing it to be an accidental whim
of nature. It was beyond me to imagine
anything else. But I soon had cause to
change my mind.

After giving my shell a thorough
examination, I returned to the rose-
bed to see if there were any more to be
found. I did not have to search for long.
With every stroke of the pick-axe, with

every lift of the spade, another shell came to light. Now that I knew what I was looking for, I found shells everywhere, where previously I had only seen stones and sand. In half an hour I collected over a hundred, after which I stopped counting. I would have needed more eyes to see them all.

Full of growing foreboding, even though, dear reader, I dared not acknowledge it, I went to the far end of the garden and began to dig there, too. To start with I found only earth and lime. But half a metre down I struck the shell-stones. I dug in a third and fourth, a fifth and sixth place. Everywhere – sometimes at the first stroke of the spade, sometimes at greater depth – I found shells, shell-stones, and shell-sand.

During the following weeks, I made excursions into the surrounding area. First I dug in Passy, then in Boulogne and Versailles, until finally I had systematically dug my way through the whole of Paris from St Cloud to Vincennes, from Gentilly to Montmorency, without once failing in my search for shells. Even when there were no shells, I found sand or stones which were materially identical. Along the course of the Seine and the Marne, the shells lay in profusion on the gravel banks; while at Charenton – where my labours were watched suspiciously by a guard from the local lunatic asylum – I had to dig a shaft to the depth of five metres before I made a strike. From every dig, I brought a few specimen shells and samples of the surrounding rocks back to my house, where I conscientiously examined them. In every case, the result of this research was exactly the same as with that of my first shell. The various shells in my collection exhibited no differences whatever, even in size; and, except for their shape, no difference from the stones to which they cleaved. This conclusion to my investigations and excursions prompted two fundamental questions, to which I both feared and longed to find the answer.

First: How far do the shells extend under the ground?

And secondly: How and why do the shells originate? Or, in other words, what causes an amorphous piece of stone – something of entirely arbitrary shape – to take on the elaborate form of a shell?

Reader, you may be inclined to interrupt me here to point out that such questions have already been discussed long ago by the great Aristotle, and that the occurrence of shell-stone is neither an original nor a surprising discovery; rather a phenomenon that has been familiar for a thousand years. To which I can only reply: Not so fast, my friend, not so fast!

I am far from claiming to be the first man to have found a petrified shell. Anyone with an eye for nature will have seen them. But no one has devoted so much thought and logical reflection to them as I have. Naturally I am familiar with the writings of the Greek philosophers concerning the origins of our planet, the continents and landscape, etc., which have a bearing on the discovery of petrified shells. After I had concluded the practical side of my research, I placed a Paris order for every book that might cast any light on the shell problem. I trawled through texts on cosmology, minerology, geology, astronomy and all related subjects. I read authors who had anything to say about shells from Aristotle to Albertus Magnus, from Theophrastus to Grosseteste, and from Avicenna to Leonardo.

What emerged from this was that while these mighty intellects exhibited ample knowledge of the incidence of shells and their appearance, structure, and distribution, when it came to their origin, their inner being, and the real

23

purpose of their existence, these writers had nothing to say.

After my study of the texts, I at any rate could answer the question of how far shells had taken over the Earth. On the principle that there is no need to sail round the world to ascertain that that sky is blue, I had already arrived at the assumption that shells appear wherever you dig a hole to look for them. I read not only of shell finds in Europe and the breadths of Asia from the highest peaks to the deepest river valleys, but also of shell-lime, shell-sand, shell-stones, and cultivated shells which were to be detected in the newly discovered continents of North and South America. All this confirmed what I had feared from my reading of the Paris texts: namely that our whole planet has been undermined by shells and their cognate substances. That what we perceive as the real world – meadows and woodland, lakes and seas, gardens, fields, barren land and fertile plains – all this amounts to no more than a pleasing but insubstantial cloak over an obdurate core. If this thin cloak were removed, our planet would be seen as a grey-white ball, assembled and developed from myriad of petrified shells, each the size of a *louis d'or*. On such a planet, no life could survive.

One might dismiss the discovery that the world consists essentially of shells as a trivial curiosity, if it referred to a stable, unaltering state of affairs. Unfortunately, this is not the case. My exhaustive studies, which impending mortality prevents me from describing

in detail, revealed that the petrification
of the world is a rapidly advancing and
unstoppable process. In our own time
the earthly cloak is showing signs of
fragility and fracture on all sides. In
many places it is already chewed up
and eaten away. Thus, we learn from
the ancient authors that the island of
Sicily, the North Coast of Africa, and
the Iberian peninsula ranked as the
most blessedly fertile in the antique
world. Today, as everyone knows,
these same regions consist – with a
few exceptions – of dust, sand, and
stones, which represent the prelimin-
ary stage of shell formation. The same
applies to most of Arabia and North
Africa; and, according to the latest
reports, to previously unexplored
areas of America. And even in our

own country, which we generally view as a land of particular excellence, there is proof of the same incessant process. Thus, in Western Provence and the South Cevennes, the cloak has been reduced to the thickness of a finger. Altogether the surface of the globe that has already fallen victim to petrification considerably exceeds the area of Europe.

The cause for the inexorable spread of shells and shell substances lies in the inexorable circulation of water. For, just as the ocean supplies living shells with their normal habitat, so water proves to be the closest ally, indeed the native element of shell-stones. As every educated person knows, water describes an endless cycle in which, through the rays of the sun, it is drawn up from the sea and gathers itself into clouds which are then carried by the wind to fall as raindrops on the land. There it fills and pervades the earth down to the smallest particle, until, converging in springs and rivulets, it swells into brooks and rivers and so makes its way back to the sea. Water makes its most fatal contribution to the spread of shells at the stage where it penetrates the earth. Through saturation, the earth is gradually dispersed, broken up, and washed away. The water then seeps down until it reaches the shell stratum where, enriched with what it has absorbed from the soil, it delivers the nourishment necessary for the shells' development. In this way, the earth's surface is forever thinning while the shell-layer continues its ceaseless growth. Anyone can confirm my discovery by boiling water from a well in a saucepan. A whiteish deposit will form on the base and sides of the pan. And in pans that are repeatedly put to this use, the deposit develops to a considerable thickness. If one breaks off the crust and grinds it in a mortar, it yields the same powder that results from shell-stones. On the other hand, if one makes the same experiment with rainwater it produces no deposit.

My unknown reader will by now have grasped the desperate situation facing the world: that water, without which we could not survive for a single day, destroys the basis of our existence, the earth, and acts as the ally of our deadly enemy, the shell. Thus the transformation of the earth's life-giving elements into the stony instruments of our destruction occurs as inescapably and irresistibly as the metamorphosis of nature's blossoming variety into the unvaried form of a shell. Let us entertain no more false notions about the end of the world. It is as certain as sunrise and sunset, as rising clouds and falling rain, that we will end in total petrification. I shall describe this process in detail on a later page. Before that, I must meet the objections that will be raised against me, and which I understand all too well. No man wants to acknowledge the worst, and fear devises a thousand ifs and buts. It is the duty only of the philosopher to take truth alone as his guide.

But, as I have already indicated, how

miserably our revered philosophers
have failed when it comes to explain-
ing the shell phenomenon. Many of
them make light of it, and maintain it
to be no more than an accidental freak
of nature; which, for some reason or
other, has imprinted stones with the
form of shells. To any intelligent person, this superficially consoling explanation – much promulgated to this day
by Italian authors – will appear so
absurdly unscientific that I can spare
myself the trouble of discussing it.

A second view, which deserves to be
taken more seriously (as it has been by
great philosophers), maintains that in
prehistory the ocean covered the entire
world, and that when it retreated the
living shells were left behind. As proof
of this assertion, every scholar relies on

the biblical account of the Flood, where indeed it is stated as fact that the whole earth up to its highest peaks was covered by water. However illuminating this interpretation may seem to the uninitiated, I must energetically contest it from my informed vantage point. We read in the Book of Moses that the world was submerged for a total of three hundred and seventy days, and that the mountain peaks – where there were as many shells as on the plains – were covered for just a hundred and fifty days. How, I enquire, could a flood of such brief duration succeed in stranding such huge numbers as we find today? And in any case, the antediluvian shells of many thousand years must long before have been ground down and turned to sand by the weather. Even if, by some inexplicable means, they had been preserved, that still fails to account for the proven fact of their continuing increase. It thus emerges that every interpretation and explanation of the nature of shells, apart from my own, is baseless.

So far we have seen that the surface of our planet is subject to a continuous conversion from its manifold materials into the substance of shells. This bring us closer to the assumption that petrification represents a general principle governing not only the earth itself but all earthly life, every thing and being in the world, and indeed in the entire cosmos.

One look through a telescope convinced me long ago that our closest neighbour in the universe, the moon, offers a virtually classical example of cosmological petrification. Indeed, it has already reached the stage now facing the earth: namely the fully completed conversion of all materials into shell-substance. Admittedly there are astronomers, even Court astronomers, who declare the moon to be a congenial planet, with wooded hills, gentle meadows, great lakes and oceans. It has nothing of the kind. What these dilettantes mistake for oceans are vast shell-deserts, and what they designate as mountain ranges on their lunar maps are desolate heaps of shell-stones. The same applies to other heavenly bodies.

Later generations with sharper minds and more powerful telescopes will confirm that I am right.

Even more horrifying than the petrification of the cosmos is the constant
decline of our own bodies into shell-
substance. The process is so violent that
in every case it leads inevitably to death.
While at conception the human foetus
only consists, if I may so express it, of a
clot of slime, small but still quite free of
shell-substance, it accumulates deposits
during its growth in the womb. At
birth, these are still quite soft and
supple, as one may see from the heads
of new-born babies. But within a short
space of time, the bones and brain of the
little body develop a hard stony cap, so
that the child takes on a somewhat rigid
posture. This pleases the parents, as it
makes him seem a proper little man.
They do not comprehend that it marks
the onset of petrification, and that

hardly has the little boy begun running
than he is staggering towards his certain
end. Admittedly, he enjoys an enviable
condition compared to that of an old
man. Among the old one may truly
witness the full effect of human petrification: the skin hardens, the hair snaps,
arteries, heart and brain calcify, the back
buckles; taking on the structure of a
shell, the man's whole figure bends
and curves and finally topples into the
grave as a wretched heap of stony
rubble. Even that is not the end. For
then the rain falls, its drops soak through
the earth, and the water gnaws and
dismembers him into minute frag-
ments which it then flushes down to
the shell stratum where, in the familiar
form of shell-stones, he achieves his
final rest.

Should anyone dismiss this picture as a fantasy, or accuse me of making unverified assertions, I can only ask him: Have you not observed the ossification of your own body, from year to year; how your movement has stiffened, and you have withered in body and soul. Have you forgotten how you used to jump, twist and bend when you were a child; falling and leaping up ten times a day as if there were nothing to it? Don't you remember your delicate skin, and the invincible vitality of your supple but powerful flesh? Look at yourself now! Your skin shrivelled into folds and wrinkles, your face carved into a scowl and twisted by aches and pains, your body stiff and creaking, every movement an effort, every step a decision;

37

and always the tormenting fear of falling over and smashing into pieces like a brittle clay jug. Don't you feel it? Don't you feel the shell in every fibre of your body? Don't you feel it reaching towards your heart? Your heart is already half in its embrace. Whoever denies that is lying!

I myself present the greatest and saddest example of a man destroyed by shells. Although for years I have drunk rainwater, so as to minimise the growth of shell-substance, I of all people have suffered the most devastating attack. When I began writing this bequest a few days ago I still had the free use of my left hand. In the meantime the fingers have petrified to the extent that I can no longer lay the pen down without assistance. As speech causes me acute pain which absolutely forbids dictation, I am now compelled to write from the wrist with accompanying pushing and pulling motions of the whole arm. My exceptionally rapid petrification is no accident. I have occupied myself with shells for so long, and wrested so many secrets from them, that they have singled me out among all other men for a particularly cruel end. For although they face no threat to their power, they are in danger of losing their secret, which they guard with revengeful pride.

You may be surprised, unknown reader, to hear me speaking of these apparently lifeless stone-like things as beings capable of relating to a particular man and seeking vengeance on him. I shall therefore initiate you into the final

and most appalling secret of the shell-
water, by which you run the manifest
danger of meeting a fate like mine.

From the very beginning of my experi-
ence of shells, I had wondered why a
stone consisting of shell material should
then go on to assume the invariable
form of a shell. As usual, the philosophers who have tried to answer this all-
important question leave us in the
lurch. The only discussion of a *vis
lapidificativa* comes from the Arab wri-
ter Avicenna, but even he can tell us
nothing of the source of this power nor
why it expresses itself in this manner. I,
on the other hand, soon became convinced that behind the universal process of petrification there stood not
only some unspecified power, but a

directly animating force acting in obe-
dience to a single higher Will. But,
convinced as I was of its existence –
having recognised its emanation
through the fossilised shells – it was
beyond me to imagine the being from
which this Will derived. What kind of
a being can one picture, that is set on
stifling the human race, making a desert
of the world, and transforming heaven
and earth into an ocean of stone?

I meditated for a full year. I locked
myself away in my study and racked my
brains. I went back to nature in the
hope of finding inspiration. All in vain.
Finally, I have to confess that I found
myself imploring this accursed unknown being for some sign of recogni-
tion. But nothing happened. My
thoughts revolved in the same old

tracks and life followed its old tormenting course: I was beginning to think
that poor Mussard would go down to
the shells, as far as the rest of mankind
from understanding the final truth.

But then something amazing happened. I must describe it, and yet I
cannot describe it, for it occupies a
sphere, so to speak, that lies above
and beyond the sphere of words. I
will try to explain the inexplicable
and to describe the indescribable, in
their effect on me. Whether I make
myself understood depends not least on
you, my unknown reader, who have
followed me thus far. I know that you
will understand me if you have the will
to do so.

It happened on an early summer day
a year ago. The weather was lovely and

the garden was in full bloom. The scent
of roses accompanied me on my walk,
and the birds sang as though trying to
convince the whole world that they
were immortal, and that this was not
one of their last summers before the
coming of the shells. It was about
midday in the blazing sun. I sat down
to rest on the bench, half in the shadow
of an apple tree. In the distance I heard
the splashing of the fountain. I felt tired
and closed my eyes. Suddenly the
sound of the fountain seemed to grow
louder until it swelled into a roar. Then
it happened. I was carried away from
my garden and out into darkness. I had
no idea of where I might be. I was
surrounded by a darkness filled with
unearthly gurglings and roaring, together with sounds of crunching and

grinding. It seemed to me at that moment, if I dare so express it, that these two groups of sounds – the roaring waters and the crunch of stone – were those of the creation of the world. I was afraid. And at the height of my fear, I began falling through the darkness until the sounds grew distant and I emerged into blinding light. I continued falling through the light, away from the dark place which I now perceived as a monstrous mass of blackness. The further I fell, the more I could see of its vast extent; and at last I recognised the black mass as a shell. It then split into two parts, opening its black wings like some gigantic bird, until they covered the whole universe, and descended over me, over the world and everything that exists, over the light, and closed together in an eternal night, leaving only the pandemonium of roaring and crunching.

The gardener found me lying on the gravel path. I had tried to get up from the bench and collapsed from exhaustion. I was carried into the house and put into bed, never to get up again. I was so enfeebled that the doctor feared for my life. Not for three weeks did I make a partial recovery. What remains from that day is a clenching pain in my stomach, which intensifies day by day and steadily extends itself through the rest of my body. This is the shell disease, which has made an exemplary case of me, marking me out from the rest of humanity as the man who has seen the Shell. I have a bitter price to pay for my enlightenment, but I pay it

gladly, as I alone know the answer to
the final question: the power that holds
all life in its spell and drives everything
to its end, the high Will that controls
the universe and condemns it to petrification as proof of its own omni-
presence and omnipotence, all this
stems from the great First Shell from
whose inner depths I have briefly been
released so as to behold its magnitude
and terrible majesty. What I saw was a
vision of the end of the world. When
the petrification of the world has
advanced to the stage where mankind
is compelled to acknowledge the
power of the Shell; when men, ex-
posed in their impotence and terror,
cry aloud to their gods for help and
deliverance, the only answer of the
Great Shell will be to open its wings

and close them over the world, and grind everything into itself.

Now that I have told you everything, my unknown reader, what is there left to say? How can I comfort you? Should I drivel on like the philosophers and prophets about the immortality of the soul, the grace of a merciful God, the resurrection of the body? Should I pass the Shell off as a gracious divinity; or ape the cults of Yahveh and Allah by proclaiming human salvation through a cult of the Shell? What purpose would that serve? Why should I lie? It has been said that man cannot live without hope. That never saved anyone from dying. My concern, as I feel I shall not survive until tomorrow, is not to begin lying on my last night on earth. It is a relief finally to be coming to the end of my dying. You, my poor friend, are still in the midst of it.

Afterword by Claude Manet,
servant to Maître Mussard
Today, 30 August 1753, at the age of sixty-six, my good master, Maître Mussard, died. I found him early in the morning, sitting in bed in his usual position. I was unable to close his eyes as their lids could not be moved. When I tried to take the pen from his hand, my master's left index-finger snapped like glass. The corpse-washer had hard work in dressing him, as his body would not relinquish its rigid sitting posture after the onset of rigor mortis. Dr Procope, my master's friend and physician, could only advise us to

order a right-angled coffin. So, on the first day of September, the horrified mourners at the Passy cemetery witnessed a right-angled grave, in which my master was showered with a thousand roses and consigned to his last rest. May God take mercy on his soul.

Translated by Irving Wardle

A NOTE ON THE AUTHOR

Patrick Süskind is the author of
Perfume, *The Pigeon* and *The Story of Mr
Sommer*. He lives in Munich.

Jimmy and the Desperate Woman, D. H. Lawrence
Einstein's Dreams, Alan Lightman
Bright Lights, Big City, Jay McInerney
Debatable Land, Candia McWilliam
Bliss and Other Stories, Katherine Mansfield
The Garden Party and Other Stories, Katherine Mansfield
So Far from God, Patrick Marnham
Lies of Silence, Brian Moore
The Lonely Passion of Judith Hearne, Brian Moore
The Pumpkin Eater, Penelope Mortimer
Lives of Girls and Women, Alice Munro
The Country Girls, Edna O'Brien
Coming Through Slaughter, Michael Ondaatje
The English Patient, Michael Ondaatje
In the Skin of a Lion, Michael Ondaatje
Running in the Family, Michael Ondaatje
Let Them Call it Jazz, Jean Rhys
Wide Sargasso Sea, Jean Rhys
Keepers of the House, Lisa St Aubin de Téran
The Quantity Theory of Insanity, Will Self
The Pigeon, Patrick Süskind
The Heather Blazing, Colm Tóibín
Cocktails at Doney's and Other Stories, William Trevor
The Choir, Joanna Trollope
Angel, All Innocence, Fay Weldon
Oranges are not the only fruit, Jeanette Winterson
The Passion, Jeanette Winterson
Sexing the Cherry, Jeanette Winterson
In Pharaoh's Army, Tobias Wolff
This Boy's Life, Tobias Wolff
Orlando, Virginia Woolf
A Room of One's Own, Virginia Woolf